Happy Birthday, Strawberry Shortcake!

By Molly Kempf

Illustrated by Tonja and John Huxtable

Grosset & Dunlap

AMERICAN GREETINGS
American Greetings with rose logo is a trademark of AGC, Inc.

GROSSET & DUNLAP
Published by the Penguin Group
Penguin Group (USA) Inc., 375 Hudson Street, New York, New York 10014, USA
Penguin Group (Canada), 90 Eglinton Avenue East, Suite 700, Toronto, Ontario M4P 2Y3, Canada
(a division of Pearson Penguin Canada Inc.)
Penguin Books Ltd., 80 Strand, London WC2R 0RL, England
Penguin Group Ireland, 25 St. Stephen's Green, Dublin 2, Ireland
(a division of Penguin Books Ltd.)
Penguin Group (Australia), 250 Camberwell Road, Camberwell, Victoria 3124, Australia
(a division of Pearson Australia Group Pty. Ltd.)
Penguin Books India Pvt. Ltd., 11 Community Centre, Panchsheel Park, New Delhi—110 017, India
Penguin Group (NZ), 67 Apollo Drive, Rosedale, North Shore 0745, Auckland, New Zealand
(a division of Pearson New Zealand Ltd.)
Penguin Books (South Africa) (Pty.) Ltd., 24 Sturdee Avenue,
Rosebank, Johannesburg 2196, South Africa

Penguin Books Ltd., Registered Offices: 80 Strand, London WC2R 0RL, England

ISBN 978-0-448-44714-8   10 9 8 7 6 5 4 3 2 1

It was a beautiful morning in Strawberryland, and Strawberry Shortcake and her pets Custard and Pupcake were out enjoying the sunshine.

"Strawberry, have you decided what to do for your birthday?" asked Custard.

"Yup," Strawberry answered. "I'm going to have a big party for all of my friends!"

"Now that I am a year older, I should have a berry grown-up party. Don't you agree, Pupcake?" Strawberry asked.

Pupcake replied by barking happily.

Strawberry spent the rest of the day planning the perfect party. *No more silly games, funny hats, or birthday cake,* she thought. *Instead I'll have music, dancing, and fancy party food.* Strawberry even sent out special grown-up invitations.

Finally the day of Strawberry's birthday arrived. She woke up extra early to get everything ready for her party. She hung the decorations, set out the food, and turned on some music. When Strawberry was done, she put on her most grown-up party dress.

Everything was perfect.

Soon all of her friends arrived ready to celebrate.

"Happy Birthday, Strawberry!" Blueberry Muffin exclaimed. "I can't wait to play musical chairs."

"And I can't wait for the piñata," added Huckleberry Pie.

"Don't forget pin the tail on the donkey," said Ginger Snap.

"I thought maybe we could listen to music instead of playing games—I just got a brand-new CD," said Strawberry.
"Oh. That could be fun, too," Ginger said.

Everyone sat down to listen to the [n]est CD from The Tutti Fruttis. It was a [ve]ry good CD, but Strawberry couldn't [hel]p but think it would be more fun if [the]y were playing musical chairs.

"Is there a piñata?" Huck asked.

"No," Strawberry answered. "I thought we were getting too old for piñatas. We could dance instead."

"Dancing *is* more grown-up," Angel Cake agreed.

The friends took turns showing off their best dance moves.

"This is berry fun!" Blueberry giggled as she twirled across the room.

We've already listened to music and danced. I wonder what else people do at grown-up parties, Strawberry thought as the song ended. I know—dessert!

"Who wants dessert?" Strawberry asked.
"I do!" Angel exclaimed. "I love birthday cake!"
"Oh, we're not having cake," Strawberry said. "I made chocolate mousse—it seemed more grown-up."

Strawberry brought out the dessert as everyone sang "Happy Birthday."

Angel looks so sad that there's no cake, Strawberry thought. And I do kind of wish that I could have blown out birthday candles. Maybe this party was a mistake.

"Are you all having a good time?" Strawberry asked nervously.

"Well, it's different from our usual parties, but it's still fun," Huck answered.

"Of course," Blueberry added. "We always have fun with you. Why?"

"Because this party isn't as fun as I thought it would be!" said Strawberry. "I like dancing and listening to music, but I really miss playing regular party games and having balloons and a big birthday cake!"

"We're all growing up, but that doesn't mean we have to be *completely* grown-up yet," Orange Blossom said, hugging her friend. "I still like playing games and eating cake, too!"

"But it's too late now," Strawberry said sadly. "The party is almost over."

"Don't worry!" Angel exclaimed. "It's not too late. I know just what we can do."

Angel, Blueberry, Ginger, and Huck all rushed to put Angel's plan into action. Angel went home and made a cake. Ginger grabbed some balloons and confetti, and Huck and Blueberry rounded up everyone's berry favorite party games.

They met back at Strawberry's house and got everything ready. Strawberry was berry excited—this was the party she really wanted!

"Here's the piñata," said Huck. "I think the birthday girl should go first!"

"I'm ready," Strawberry said as she tied on a blindfold.

Ginger and Blueberry played pin the
on the donkey as Strawberry took
first swing at the piñata.
"Now *this* is a party!" exclaimed Huck.

Then Angel walked in carrying a cake topped with birthday candles. "Make a wish, Strawberry," she said.

Strawberry took a deep breath and blew out all of her candles.

"I already got my wish," she said with a smile. "The best birthday with the berry best friends I could ever ask for!"